THREE SACKS OF TRUTH

a story from France

adapted by
ERIC A. KIMMEL
illustrated by
ROBERT RAYEVSKY

Holiday House
New York

To Sue and Mort Malter

E.A.K.

This story was adapted from "The Three May Peaches," the first story in Paul Delarue's *Borzoi Book of French Folk Tales*.

E.A.K.

Printed in the United States of America

First Edition
Library of Congress Cataloging-in-Publication Data
Kimmel, Eric A.
Three sacks of truth : a story from France / adapted by
Eric A. Kimmel ; illustrated by Robert Rayevsky.—1st ed.
p. cm.
Summary: With the aid of a perfect peach, a silver fife,
and his own resources, Petit Jean outwits a dishonest king
and wins the hand of a princess.
ISBN 0-8234-0921-X
[1. Fairy tales. 2. Folklore—France.] I. Rayevsky, Robert,
ill. II. Title.
PZ8.K527Th 1993 91-19265 CIP AC
398.21'0944—dc20
[E]

Once upon a time there was a king who was a good deal less honest than a king ought to be. Whatever he gave with his right hand, he took back with his left.

This king had a craving for peaches. One day he announced, "I will marry my daughter to the man who brings me the perfect peach." His daughter was known far and wide as a princess of exquisite charm, so in no time at all the roads were choked with suitors from all over the kingdom carrying peaches of every description. However, no peach was ever quite perfect. They were either too sweet or too sour, too hard or too soft, too ripe or not ripe enough. In truth, the king had no intention of marrying his daughter to anybody. It was all a trick to allow him to eat his fill of peaches without having to pay for a single one.

In a far corner of the kingdom lived a widow and her three sons: Pierre, Pascal, and Jean. Jean's brothers called him Petit Jean because he was so small. However, he was the cleverest by far. A peach tree grew in the widow's garden. Every morning, rain or shine, she sprinkled it with holy water. The tree grew full and tall. It blossomed once every ten years and brought forth only three peaches. But they were absolutely perfect.

When the widow heard of the king's decree, she plucked one of the peaches, put it in a basket, and covered it with a napkin. She handed the basket to her son Pierre, saying, "Take this peach to the king. With luck, you will marry his daughter and make your fortune."

Pierre set out, carrying the basket. Along the way he passed a holy well. An old woman sitting beside the well called out to him, "Good day to you, young man. What, pray tell, do you have in your basket?"

"Frogs and toads," Pierre answered rudely.

"So it is," the old woman replied. She said nothing more, and Pierre walked on. But when he came before the king and lifted up the napkin, lo and behold, his basket was full to the brim with hopping frogs and toads! "Throw him out!" the king ordered. So Pierre was tossed in the street and had to make his way home with nothing to show for his efforts.

Undaunted, the widow plucked the second peach, put it in a basket, covered it with a napkin, and gave it to her son Pascal, saying, "Now it is your turn. Where your brother has failed, you may perhaps succeed."

Pascal set out with the peach. Along the way he passed the same holy well. The old woman sitting beside it called out to him, "Good day, young man. What, pray tell, do you have in your basket?"

"Snakes and lizards," Pascal answered.

"So it is," the woman replied. Pascal continued on. But when he came before the king and lifted up the napkin, what did he find in his basket but a slithering, squirming mass of snakes and lizards!

"Throw him out!" cried the king. So Pascal, like Pierre, ended up in the street and had to make his way home empty-handed, with nothing to show for his journey.

One peach remained. The widow plucked it from the tree, put it in a basket, covered it with a napkin, and gave it to her third son, Petit Jean. She told him, "You are cleverer than your brothers. Keep your wits about you, be polite to all you meet, and sure luck will follow you."

Petit Jean set out with the basket over his arm. Along the way he passed the holy well.

"Good day to you, grandmother dear," he called to the old woman sitting beside it.

"And good day to you," she replied. "What do you have in your basket?"

"One perfect peach," Petit Jean answered.

"So it is," the old woman replied. Then she took a silver fife from her apron and handed it to Petit Jean. "If the king goes back on his word, play on this fife. You will come to a good end if you keep your wits about you."

Petit Jean thanked the old woman and continued on. When he arrived at the palace the king asked him, "What, pray tell, do you have in your basket?"

"One perfect peach," Petit Jean replied. He lifted the napkin, and there it lay: the most perfect peach that ever grew on a tree.

"I must have a taste," the king cried. One bite sent him swooning with ecstasy. "It is perfection itself!" he exclaimed. At once he realized his error. His saying those words gave Petit Jean the right to marry the princess.

The king could not break his promise, but he could tie it in knots. He told Petit Jean, "Before you can marry my daughter, there is something else you must do. I have ten thousand rabbits. You must take them out to the meadow and bring them back in the evening. If you can do that for four days running without losing a rabbit, you can marry my daughter. But if one rabbit is missing, out you go."

Petit Jean thought a while. Then he said, "I have herded sheep and goats. Rabbits can't be too hard to manage."

Petit Jean went down to the rabbit pen the next morning. As soon as he opened the gate, the ten thousand rabbits went hopping over hill and dale. Unconcerned, Petit Jean continued on to the meadow, where he spent the day resting on the grass. When evening came, he took out the silver fife the old woman had given him and played a melody.

At the first note the rabbits lifted their ears. At the second, they scampered back to the meadow. At the third, amazing to tell, they formed themselves like soldiers into lines and columns.

"Forward march!" Petit Jean said. And off they went.

The king could not believe his eyes when he saw Petit Jean leading the rabbits home like a fifer leading a regiment. "Are they all here?" he asked.

"Count them," Petit Jean replied. Sure enough, not a single rabbit was missing.

The king rubbed his forehead. This problem was greater than he anticipated. The next morning, as soon as Petit Jean let out the rabbits, he sent for his daughter.

"Go to the meadow disguised as a kitchen maid and ask Petit Jean for one of his rabbits. Pay whatever he asks, then bring the rabbit to me. And make no mistakes, unless you fancy yourself married to a peach peddler."

Now in truth, the princess fancied exactly that, for she liked the way Petit Jean winked at her when he led the rabbits home. However, being a dutiful daughter, she put on a kitchen maid's apron and hurried to the meadow.

She found Petit Jean lying on the grass, with rabbits here and there. He held one in his lap. "How much are your rabbits?" the princess asked.

"I will let you have this one for seven kisses," Petit Jean said to her.

"Oh, very well," said the princess, blushing. She gave Petit Jean his seven kisses, tucked the rabbit in her apron, and started on her way home.

Before she arrived, it came time to round up the rabbits. Petit Jean blew on his fife. At the first note, the rabbit in the princess's apron lifted its ears. At the second, it bounded back to the meadow. At the third, it fell into line with the other rabbits so that when Petit Jean led them home that evening, there they were, all ten thousand, and not one single rabbit was missing.

The next morning the king summoned the queen. "Go to the meadow disguised as a cook and ask Petit Jean what he wants for one of his rabbits. Pay any price, but make sure the bunny doesn't escape."

The queen put on her disguise and hurried to the meadow. "How much are your rabbits?" she asked Petit Jean.

"They are not for sale, but I will give you one if you will stand on your head while I count to three," said Petit Jean.

The queen blushed purple. However, the king had told her to pay any price, so she stood on her head with her petticoats tumbling about her ears while Petit Jean counted one, two, three. "Here is your bunny," he said, handing her a fine, fat rabbit.

The queen took the rabbit home and locked it in the tallest tower of the palace. "To escape from here it will have to fly," she said.

But at the first note of Petit Jean's fife, the rabbit hopped to the window. On the second, it wriggled through the bars. On the third it flew from the tower, vaulted over the wall, and took its place in line just as Petit Jean led the rabbits home.

"Are they all here?" the king asked.

"Count them," Petit Jean said. To the king's chagrin, not a single one was missing.

The king decided to handle matters himself. The next day, disguised as a peddler, he saddled a donkey and rode out to the meadow.

"How much are these rabbits?" the king asked Petit Jean.

"I don't sell them; they have to be earned."

"What must I do to earn one?"
"Kiss your donkey," Petit Jean said.

The king hemmed and hawed, but in the end he placed his lips on the donkey's mouth and gave it a smacking kiss. Petit Jean gave him a rabbit.

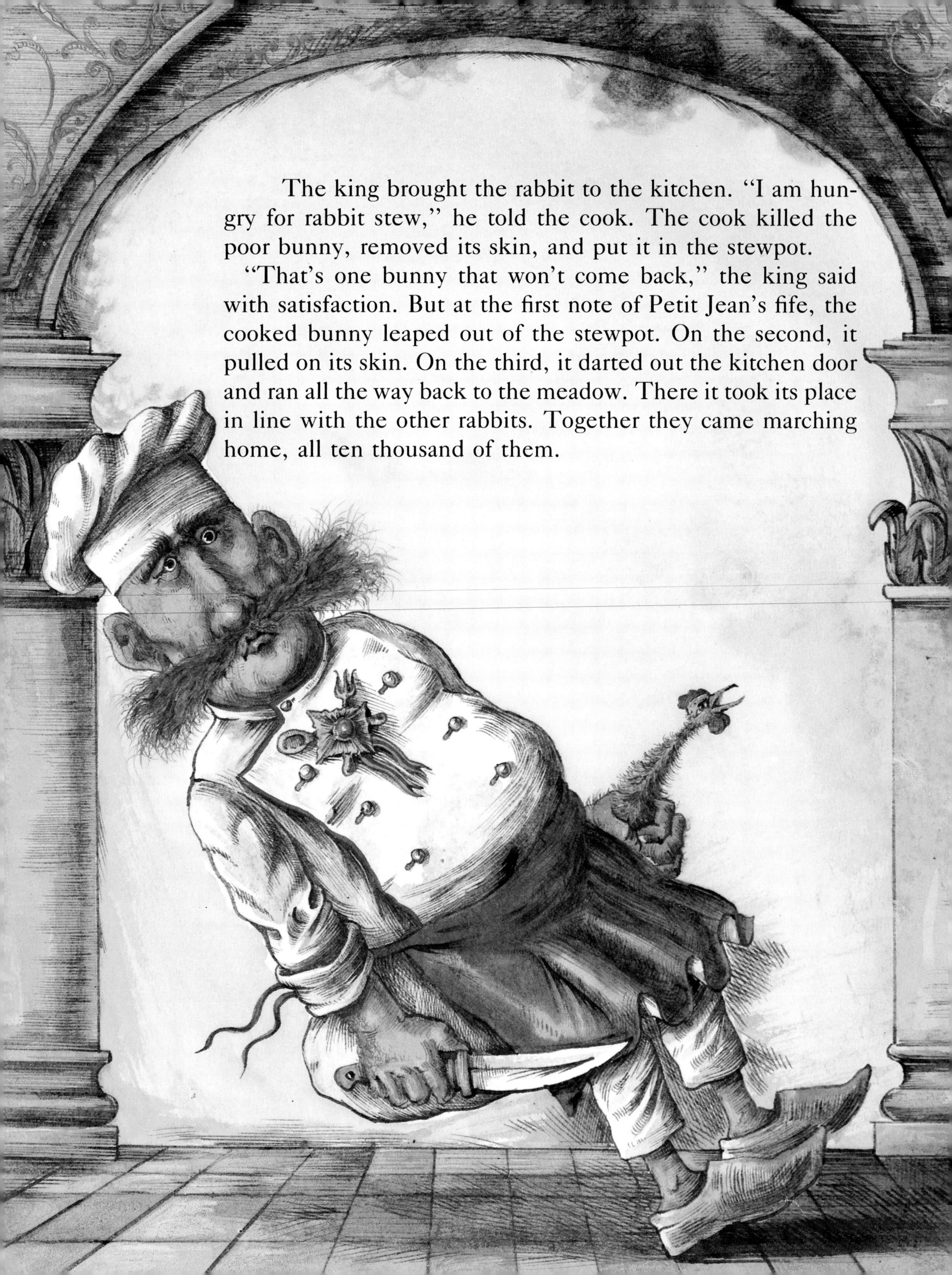

The king brought the rabbit to the kitchen. "I am hungry for rabbit stew," he told the cook. The cook killed the poor bunny, removed its skin, and put it in the stewpot.

"That's one bunny that won't come back," the king said with satisfaction. But at the first note of Petit Jean's fife, the cooked bunny leaped out of the stewpot. On the second, it pulled on its skin. On the third, it darted out the kitchen door and ran all the way back to the meadow. There it took its place in line with the other rabbits. Together they came marching home, all ten thousand of them.

Petit Jean then said to the king, "I have herded your rabbits for four days without losing one. Now I want the bride you promised me."

"Not so fast," the king replied. "Before you can marry my daughter, you must show me three sacks of truth."

"I can do that," Petit Jean said. "But you must assemble your court first. These sacks hold great truths, and I want everyone to hear them."

With the whole court assembled, Petit Jean appeared holding three flour sacks. He took the first sack and said to the princess, "Is it true that out there in the meadow you gave me seven kisses for one rabbit?"

The princess blushed, but she had to admit it was true.

"That's one truth. Into the sack you go," said Petit Jean. The princess got into the first sack. Petit Jean took the second sack and turned to the queen, "Is it true that for one rabbit

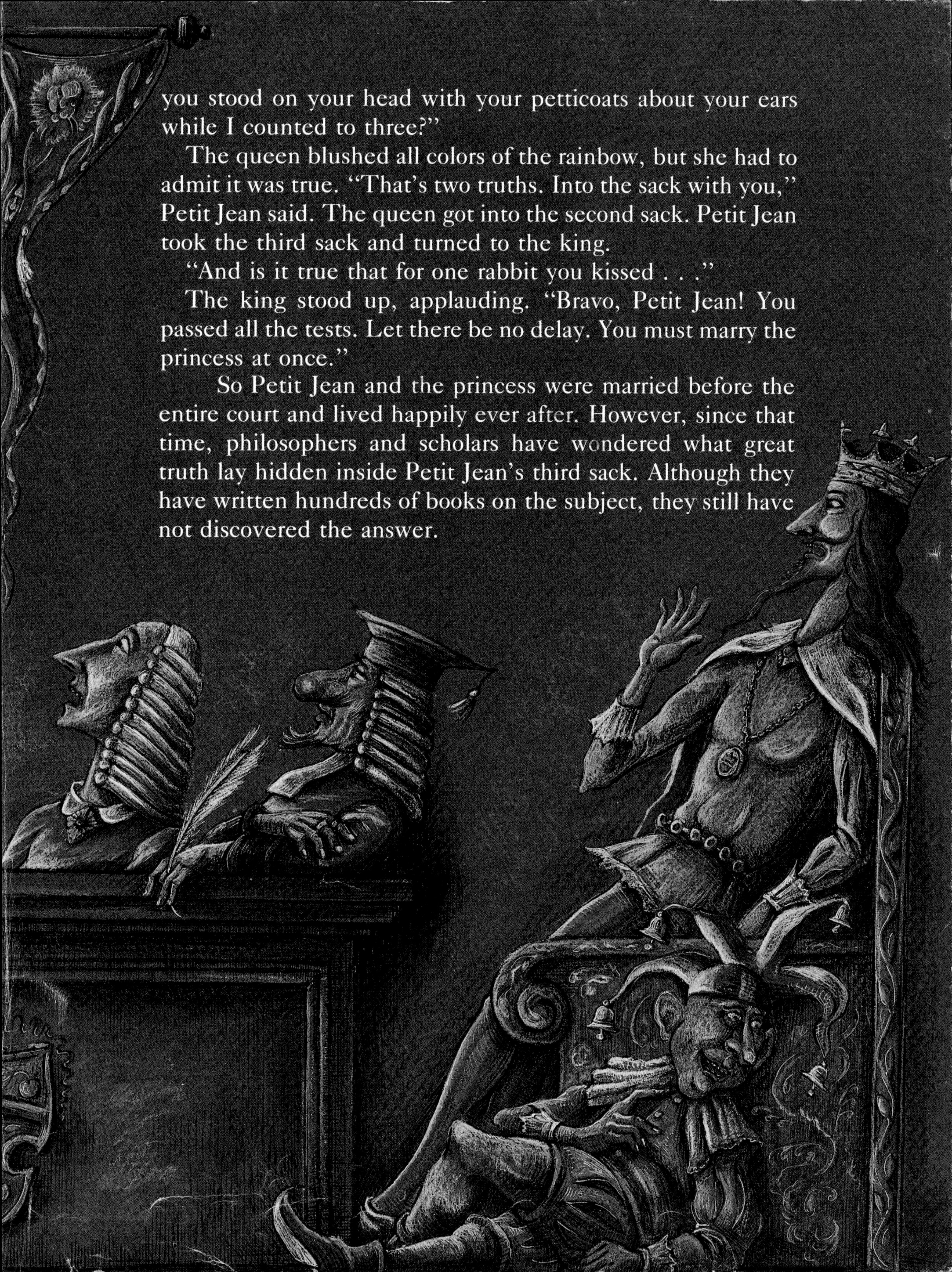

you stood on your head with your petticoats about your ears while I counted to three?"

The queen blushed all colors of the rainbow, but she had to admit it was true. "That's two truths. Into the sack with you," Petit Jean said. The queen got into the second sack. Petit Jean took the third sack and turned to the king.

"And is it true that for one rabbit you kissed . . ."

The king stood up, applauding. "Bravo, Petit Jean! You passed all the tests. Let there be no delay. You must marry the princess at once."

So Petit Jean and the princess were married before the entire court and lived happily ever after. However, since that time, philosophers and scholars have wondered what great truth lay hidden inside Petit Jean's third sack. Although they have written hundreds of books on the subject, they still have not discovered the answer.

Perhaps they never will.